The Berenstain Kids

I ♥ COLORS

Colors, colors,
wherever you look.
Learn all about them
in this book.

A FIRST TIME READER™

The Berenstain Kids

I ♥

Random House 🏠 New York

Library of Congress Cataloging-in-Publication Data: Berenstain, Stan. The Berenstain kids: I love colors. (A First time reader) SUMMARY: Two youngsters describe things that are red, blue, yellow, orange, beige, pink, and other colors. [1. Color—Fiction. 2. Stories in rhyme] I. Berenstain, Jan. II. Title. III. Series: Berenstain, Stan. First time reader. PZ8.3.B4493Bhk 1987 [E] 87-9722 ISBN: 0-394-89129-5 (trade); 0-394-99129-X (lib. bdg.)

Manufactured in the United States of America   3 4 5 6 7 8 9 0

COLORS

Stan & Jan Berenstain

Red! Red!
I love red!

The color of a fire truck.

The color of a rose.

The color of a circus clown's
funny nose.

What about yellow?
I love yellow.

The color of a lemon
and lemon pies.
The amazing color
of a hoot owl's eyes.

Don't forget blue,
good old blue.

The color of a bluebird,

a clear blue sky,

a bright blue balloon
floating by.

We love colors,
red, yellow, and blue!
Hooray for yellow,
red, and blue!

But there are other
colors too—

They come from yellow,
red, and blue.

We will show you
how it's done.
Come join us in
our color fun.

First, yellow and red.
Ready, get set—
Mix yellow and red
and what do you get?

Orange! Orange
is what you get!

We love orange!
Bright and bold!

The color of
a marigold.

ORANGES

The color of
an orange-colored fruit.

The color of Cousin
Zeke's zoot suit.

Green's nice too.
We get it by mixing
yellow and blue.

Green! Green!
We love green!
It's Mother Nature's
favorite too.
Just look around.
You'll find it's true.

Though all greens
share a name,
all greens, friends,
are not the same.

Some are dark.
Some are light.
Some are dull.
Some are bright.

This fact, friends,
is also true
of all the other
colors too.

Colors! Colors!
Dull and bright!
We love colors
dark and light!

Oops!
What about purple,
which, don't forget,
is also known as violet?

We get purple,
rich and fine,
when red and blue
we combine.

The purple of a butterfly,

the violet, so small and shy.

Jackie Horner's
purple plum
that he pulled out
with his thumb!

We love colors,
red, yellow, and blue!
We love green
and orange too!
And purple, of course—
which, don't forget,
is also known as violet!

PAINT AND HARDWARE

BUFF BEIGE

PINK TAN BROWN

Here are more—
at the paint
and hardware store!

Buff and beige,
pink, tan, and brown.
The colors of the people
in our town!

The colors of different people's skin.

The colors of the clothes
that they are in.

The sunset's colors
at the end of the day.

Now comes night.
The colors of day
all fade away.

It grows dark
and darker still.

Will colors come back?

Yes! They will!

With the sunrise
comes the dawn!
When Mother Nature turns
her colors back on!

Hooray! Another
colorful day!
We get up,
go out, and say...

We love colors,
red, yellow, and blue!
We love green
and orange too!
And purple, of course—
which, don't forget,
is also known as violet!